Your Happy Heart

How Helping Others Helps You, Too

To all the students I have been honored to teach.
Helping you heal your hearts finally healed mine.

– Amie Dean

NCYI titles may be purchased in bulk at special discounts for educational, business, fundraising, or promotional use. For more information, please email sales@ncyi.org.

NATIONAL CENTER for
YOUTH ISSUES

P.O. Box 22185
Chattanooga, TN 37422-2185
423.899.5714 • 866.318.6294
fax: 423.899.4547 • www.ncyi.org

ISBN: 978-1-937870-56-0 $9.95
Library of Congress Control Number: 2018966097
© 2018 National Center for Youth Issues, Chattanooga, TN
All rights reserved.
Written by: Amie Dean
Illustrations by: Susan Keeter
Published by National Center for Youth Issues • Softcover
Printed at Starkey Printing, Chattanooga, Tennessee, U.S.A., February 2019

"Javon, please line up," Mr. Hirsch, my fifth-grade teacher, called.

I had finally made it into the special reading group! We were going to meet our kindergarten Book Buddies today, and I was going to see my favorite teacher, Ms. Sammons. Win-win.

Ms. Sammons was really nice to me when I had all my troubles. She helped me get control of my anger, so I knew she was going to be proud to see I had been picked to be a Book Buddy.

When we arrived,
Ms. Sammons hugged me
and said, "You made it, Javon!
I've picked the perfect partner
for you." She pointed to a small
boy with dark curly hair.

"Richard, this is Javon, and he will be your Book Buddy. You're going to love him."

Richard barely turned his head around to look at me and then slowly faced the wall again. I felt kind of disappointed. Most of the other little kids jumped up and ran to their Book Buddies.

I sat down next to Richard and stuck out my fist for a bump. He was not having it. I asked him about his favorite book and favorite superhero, but no answer. He kept his head down, so I stopped asking questions and told him a few things about me.

"Ms. Sammons was my kindergarten teacher," I said. "I love to play football and basketball." "What do you like to do?" Still no answer, so I read him a book about animals.

When Ms. Sammons called time's up, I tried the fist bump again, but he didn't respond. "All right, little man, see you next week?"

Nothing. Not. One. Word.

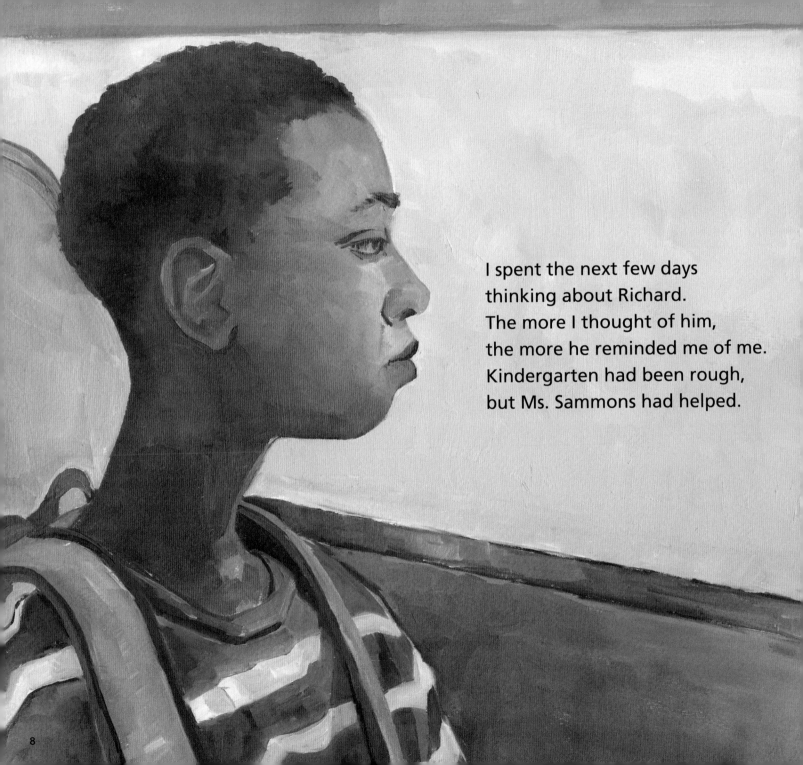

I spent the next few days
thinking about Richard.
The more I thought of him,
the more he reminded me of me.
Kindergarten had been rough,
but Ms. Sammons had helped.

She taught me about *the mads, sads,* and *happies*. She taught me that every person has these feelings. Some sad things happened to me when I was little, so sometimes I cried at school. I even hit kids and threw things.

Ms. Sammons let me go to the Zen Zone when I needed to calm down. There was a furry, stuffed puppy she called "Lucky" that I used to hold to help me calm down.

I still have Lucky. When I got home on the last day of kindergarten, I opened my backpack, and there he was. I guess Ms. Sammons thought I needed him more than she did. Sometimes I still sneak a little hug. Lucky always makes me feel better.

Tuesday came around,
and I had a plan.

When I got to Richard's class,
I took a deep breath and
walked straight to him.

"Hey little man, I'm glad you're here today. I've been thinking about you."

Silence.

Then I asked, "Have you ever been in Ms. Sammons's Zen Zone?" He picked up his head and stared at me. He said, "How do you know about that?"

"Oh, I know *all* about that," I told him. "It was like my second home." He laughed a little. My plan was working.

"Did you have *the mads,* too?" he asked.

I told him about my mads and that a little stuffed puppy named Lucky helped me find my calm place. I told him I learned some cool things that helped me feel better.

"In second grade, Mr. Sharpe, our school counselor, taught us about finding our gifts. Your gifts are what make you special, and help you feel proud of yourself. We made a list of the things we like about ourselves. Do you want to see my list?"

I unfolded the piece of paper and read:

> *I'm smart with heart.*
>
> *I run fast, too.*
>
> *I'll be me, and you be you.*

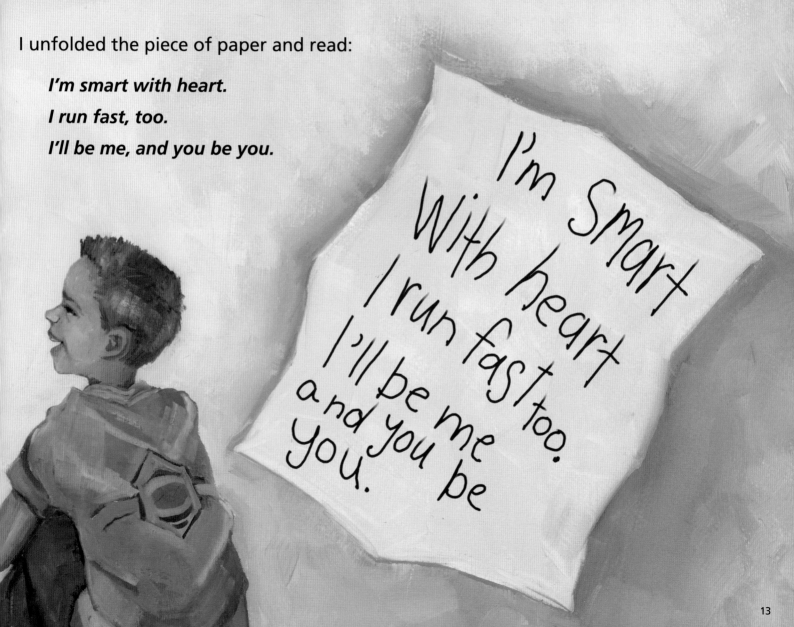

He smiled, "Hey, I'm fast too."

I gave him a piece of paper and said,
"Can you tell me a few more of your gifts?
I'll write them down for you."

He frowned. "I don't think I have any gifts."

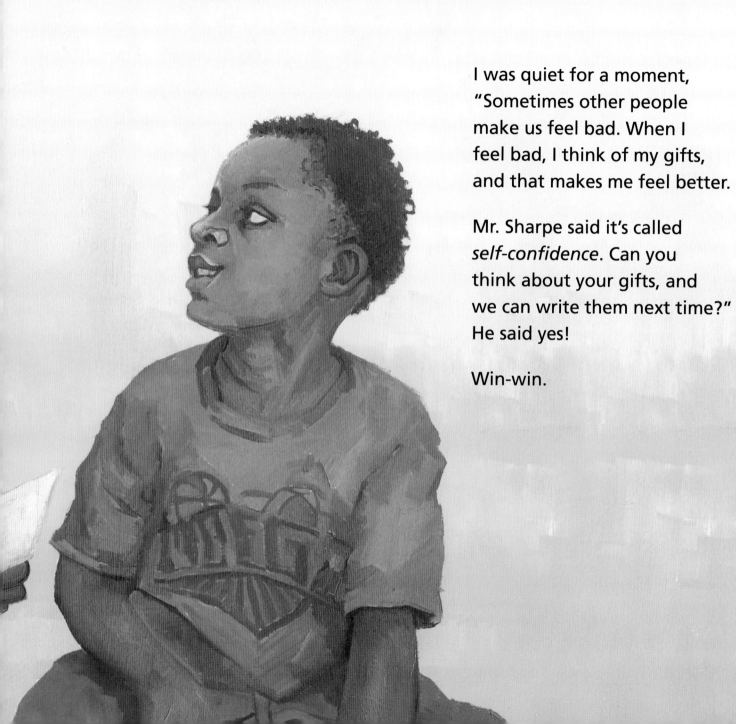

I was quiet for a moment, "Sometimes other people make us feel bad. When I feel bad, I think of my gifts, and that makes me feel better.

Mr. Sharpe said it's called *self-confidence*. Can you think about your gifts, and we can write them next time?" He said yes!

Win-win.

Every week, I went back to Ms. Sammons's room
to meet with Richard. Each time he let me read
to him, and gave me a fist bump, too.

I had something special planned for Richard for our last visit. But when I got to the room, he wasn't there. Ms. Sammons looked stressed. "Javon, Richard had to leave the classroom this morning. He's in Mr. Sharpe's office."

"Can I go talk to him? I think I can help."

She paused for a minute, "Okay, let's give it a shot."

I ran to Mr. Sharpe's office
and knocked on his door.

"Hey Javon, what's up, man?"
Mr. Sharpe asked.

"I'm here to see Richard. Is it okay if I read to him?"

"Sure, Javon. You're a good friend to Richard."

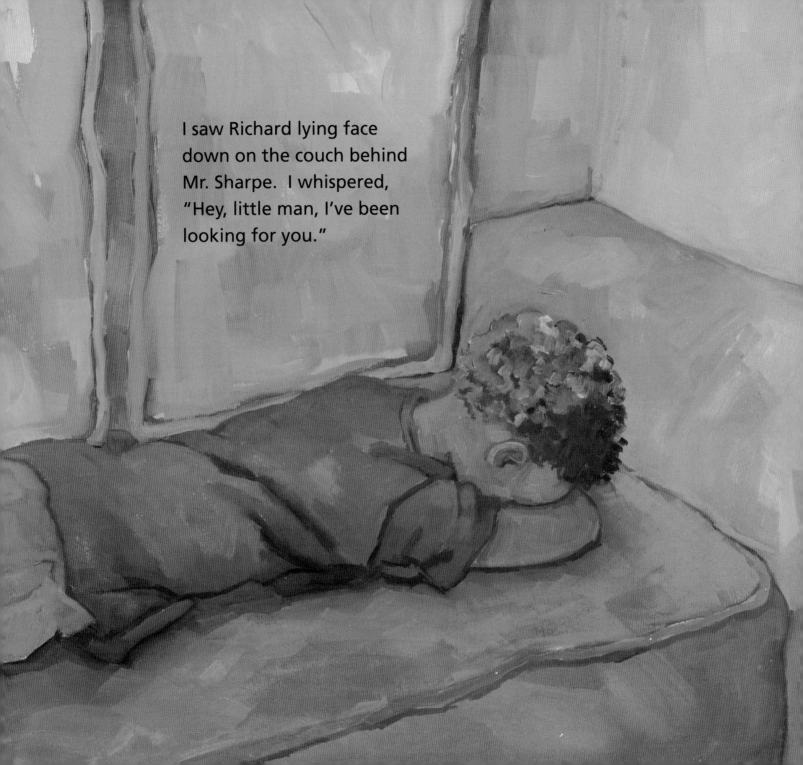

I saw Richard lying face down on the couch behind Mr. Sharpe. I whispered, "Hey, little man, I've been looking for you."

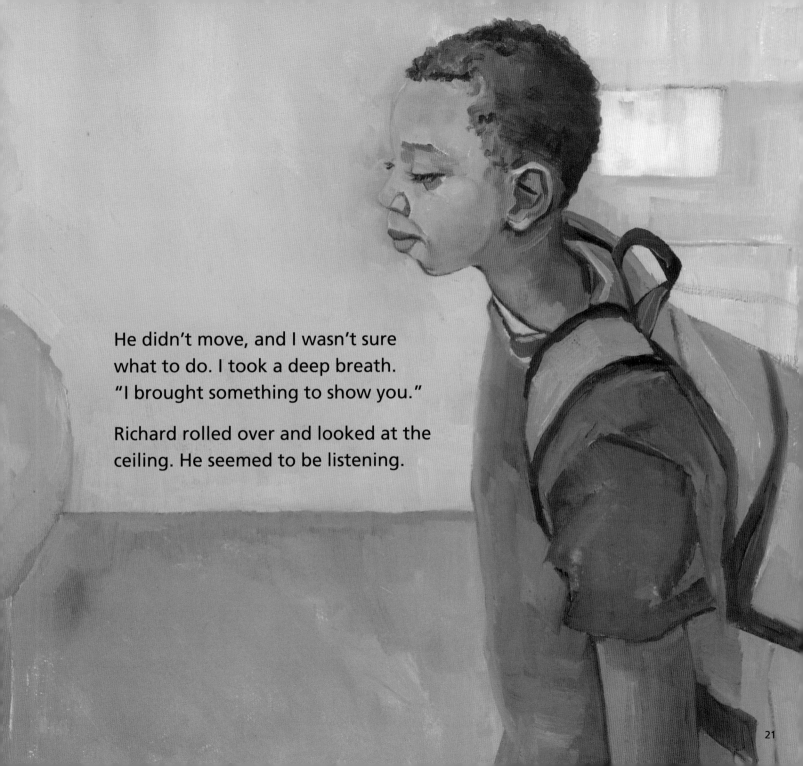

He didn't move, and I wasn't sure
what to do. I took a deep breath.
"I brought something to show you."

Richard rolled over and looked at the
ceiling. He seemed to be listening.

"Last year we drew a heart in art class,
and our teacher told us to put three things
in our heart that make us happy. Each of
these things makes me feel calm when I
hold them or picture them in my mind."

I showed him my heart with the Batman figure
I got when my parents were still together,
a picture of my grandma, and of course, Lucky.

Richard sat up and smiled at me.

"I made this for you so you can fill your heart with the things that make you happy. It can be anything you want."

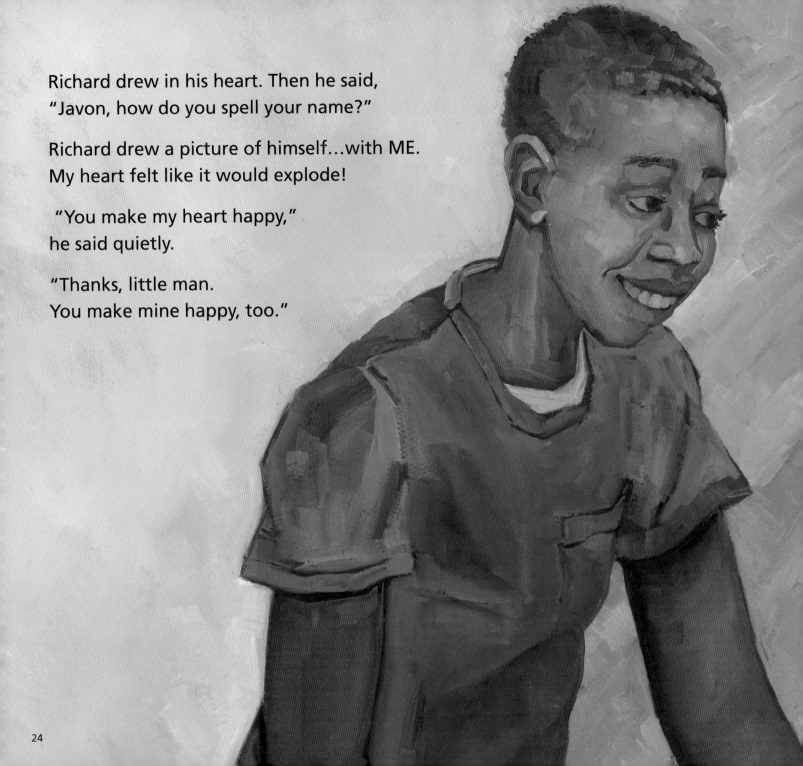

Richard drew in his heart. Then he said,
"Javon, how do you spell your name?"

Richard drew a picture of himself…with ME.
My heart felt like it would explode!

"You make my heart happy,"
he said quietly.

"Thanks, little man.
You make mine happy, too."

I reached down to get my backpack.
I unzipped it and closed my eyes as I
touched Lucky one last time.
"I brought this for you, Richard.
I think Lucky can help you —
just like he's always helped me."

"I'm going to miss you, Javon."

"I'm going to miss you too, little man.
Hold on to Lucky any time you miss me
or you're feeling sad. I promise he can
make you feel better."

Mr. Sharpe let me walk Richard back to his class.
Ms. Sammons smiled when she saw us.

"Remember what I told you—Lucky is there for you,"
I told Richard. He gave me another big hug. I am not
usually down for a hug in the hallway, but I let it slide
because I'm going to miss that little dude.

I've learned so many things at East Elementary. I can find my "Zen Zone" in lots of places. I learned it is okay to have a favorite stuffed animal to help you stay calm. I learned everyone feels angry or sad sometimes. I learned I have many gifts that make me special. But I learned the most important thing from Richard.

Helping someone find their happiness can make your own heart happy, too.

Win-win.

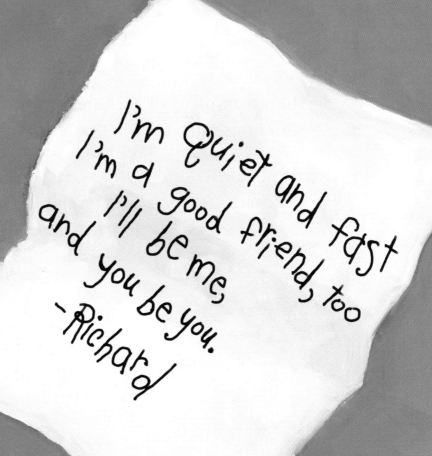

I'm quiet and fast
I'm a good friend, too
I'll be me,
and you be you.
- Richard

Tips for Helping Children Find Their Gifts

There is no greater self-confidence builder than to know who you are and understand what you have to offer the world. Yet so many of us struggle with creating a negative personal narrative which highlights the things we DON'T do well instead of the things we do.

1. **"Kindness is free to give, but priceless to receive." – RAKtivist**

   We all have gifts to give. Javon gave Richard his most prized possession, Lucky the Dog, but giving to others doesn't have to be focused on material things. Show your child that we all have gifts to share such as time, attention, love, kindness, a smile, and sometimes a physical object. We are all capable of helping others, with and without material things.

2. **Expose your children to a variety of activities.**

   They may be good at some and struggle with others. Let them know that not being the best is a human experience that allows growth and guides us in the direction of our own personal path. There are many different ways to a happy heart.

3. **Help your child make a list of things he/she loves to do.**

   These are not just talents and things they do well, but also character traits, like being kind, being helpful, being respectful, etc. Highlight three to five traits they can use in their own "I'll Be Me" poem.

4. **You can't raise positive people with negative feedback.**

   Teach your child positive self-talk. Instead of saying "I'm not a good reader," help rephrase her thinking into, "I know all of my letters and a lot of my sight words."

5. **Focus on the "Power of Yet."**

   Guide children to include **Yet** in their statements; for example, "I can't pass this class **yet**," or " I don't know how to swim **yet**." Having a growth mindset allows children to view failure as an opportunity to learn and overcome.

BREATHE

Steps for helping your child/student calm down

- **B**e Calm. Be the adult. When you act calm, you bring a sense of order to chaos.

- **R**espectful tone/language – Use it even when they don't "deserve" it. This is how they learn to behave when stressed or in crisis.

- **E**yes or Ears. Allow student to listen if eye contact is a struggle. Some students can't look you in the eye as it causes fear or stress.

- **A**SK questions. Can you try that again? What do you need? Please tell me – maybe I can help.

- **T**ake time to **listen**. It is one of the most common responses my students have given when I asked them "What does respect look like to you?"

- **H**elp when you can. If their request is reasonable, why not help?

- **E**xpect the BEST. They sense it either way.